Perfectly POPPY

Beach Bummer

Story by Michele Jakubowski

Pictures by Erica-Jane Waters

Picture Window Books

Perfectly Poppy is published by Picture Window Books, a Capstone Imprint
1710 Roe Crest Drive, North Mankato, Minnesota 56003
www.capstonepub.com

Library of Congress Cataloging-in-Publication Data
Jakubowski, Michele, author.
Perfectly Poppy beach bummer / by Michele Jakubowski ; illustrated by Erica Jane Waters.
pages cm. -- (Perfectly Poppy)
Summary: Poppy and her best friend Millie are at the beach, but Poppy is not having much fun
because she finds the water too cold, the wind too strong, and the sand too itchy.
ISBN 978-1-4795-2284-2 (hardcover) -- ISBN 978-1-4795-2358-0 (pbk.)
1. Beaches--Juvenile fiction. 2. Best friends--Juvenile fiction. [1. Beaches--Fiction. 2. Best friends--
Fiction. 3. Friendship--Fiction.] I. Waters, Erica-Jane, illustrator. II. Title. III. Title: Beach bummer.
PZ7.J153555Pe 2014
813.6--dc23   2013027852

Designers: Heather Kindseth Wutschke and Kristi Carlson

Printed in the United States of America in North Mankato, Minnesota.
092013   007766CGS14

Table of Contents

Chapter 1
Time to Unload

"We're here!" Poppy yelled as she jumped out of the car.

After a long drive with Poppy's family, Poppy and Millie were finally at the beach.

"Let's go!" Poppy yelled as she started to run toward the water.

"Not so fast," her mom called.

"You need to help carry things."

Poppy and Millie each grabbed a

beach bag. The bags were heavy, and

walking in the sand was tricky.

They helped set up the beach

umbrella, chairs, and towels.

"Done," Poppy said. "Now it's

time to swim!"

"Not so fast," said her mom again.

"Now what?" Poppy asked. She was starting to think she'd never get to swim!

"You need sunscreen," her mom said, holding up the bottle.

Poppy stood still while her mom

put sunscreen on her. It took forever!

Finally her mom was done. Poppy

asked, "Now can I swim?"

Her mom smiled and said, "Yes.

I'll come too."

Chapter 2

Beach Blues

"Hooray!" Poppy and Millie

yelled as they raced down the beach.

They had been waiting weeks to go

swimming, and it was time to have

some fun!

Poppy and Millie ran into the
water. Her mom watched.

"It's freezing!" Millie said as she
quickly ran back out of the water.

"But we have to swim!" Poppy said as she stood in the cold water.

She tried to splash around, but it wasn't fun to splash alone. Soon she began shivering. Then a big wave came and knocked her over.

This made Poppy grumpy. She

joined Millie on the beach.

"If we can't swim, what are we

supposed to do?" Poppy asked.

"We could play with the beach

ball," Millie said.

Poppy and Millie tried throwing

the ball back and forth. The wind

made it hard to catch.

Poppy chased after the ball.

She tripped in the sand and fell

on her face.

"Ugh!" Poppy shouted. The sand

was sticking to her. It was really itchy.

"I'm going to go rinse off in the showers," Poppy told her mom as she headed for the bathroom.

She walked into the dark bathroom. Poppy wrinkled her nose. "Gross!"

The floors were wet and sandy, and the room smelled fishy. In the corner was a shower.

Poppy turned on the shower. The water was freezing! She rinsed off the sand and grabbed her towel. Then she slipped and fell on the dirty floor.

Chapter 3

Sun and Smiles

Poppy wanted to have the perfect beach day, but instead it was a total beach bummer.

She was tired, dirty, and hungry. She picked herself up and went to find her mom.

Then she began crying. "I don't like the beach!"

"Oh, Poppy," her mom said as she gave her a big hug.

Poppy's mom spread her towel under the umbrella. She gave Poppy a bottle of water and some crunchy apple slices.

Then Millie came running over. "What's wrong, Poppy?" she asked.

"I want to go home," Poppy said.

"But you were so excited about

coming to the beach," her mom said.

"I know I was. But the water is too cold, and the wind is too windy," Poppy said.

"How about you play in the sand?" her mom asked.

"I tried that," Poppy said. "I fell on my face!"

"Let's build a sand castle!" Millie said. "You won't fall down doing that. It will be fun."

"I guess," Poppy said, but she wasn't so sure.

Poppy and Millie began building

their sand castle. At first it was small.

They made it bigger and bigger and

bigger. Then they collected sea shells

to decorate it. It looked great!

"This is quite a workout! I'm getting hot," Poppy said.

"Me too," said Millie. "Should we try the water again?"

"I guess we could," said Poppy.

They walked slowly into the water with Poppy's mom close by. It still felt cold, but this time the cold felt good. They began splashing and jumping around.

"Good news!" Poppy said. "My beach bummer is now a beach blast. I like the beach again!"

"What a relief!" Millie laughed as she splashed Poppy.

"You're telling me," replied Poppy with a huge smile.

Poppy's New Words

I learned so many new words today! I made sure to write them down so I could use them again.

collected (kuh-LEK-ted) — gathered things together

decorate (DEK-uh-rate) — add things to something to make it look prettier

grumpy (GRUHM-pee) — grouchy or crabby

relief (ri-LEEF) — a feeling of freedom from pain or worry

rinsed (RINSST) — washed something in clean water

shivering (SHIV-ur-ing) — shaking with cold

Poppy's Ponders

After my day at the beach, I had some time to think. Here are some of my questions and thoughts from the day.

1. I was excited to go to the beach, but then so many things went wrong. I was really disappointed. Talk about a time when you were disappointed.

2. If you were me, would you have stayed at the beach or gone home early? Why?

3. Write a paragraph about your favorite things to do at the beach.

4. I didn't have the perfect beach day, but my mom said I persevered. Persevere means to keep on trying when faced with obstacles or difficulties. Write about a time when you persevered.

Frozen Grapes

When it's hot outside, nothing tastes better than some cold treats. Here is how I make frozen grapes, which are my favorite. My mom says they are a lot healthier than Popsicles or ice cream, and they taste just as good.

What you do:

1. Rinse the grapes.

2. Dry them off.

3. Wrap the grapes in a clean kitchen dish towel.

4. Put them in the freezer for a couple of hours.

5. Take out and enjoy. Easy and delicious!

Beach Day Activities

Don't just lie around at the beach. Grab a friend and have some fun. Here are some of my favorite beach activities. Put on some sunscreen and try them out!

- build a sand castle

- jump waves

- collect sea shells

- bury feet in the sand

- skip rocks in the water

- swim, swim, swim

- play catch with a beach ball

About the Author

Raised in the Chicago suburb of Hoffman Estates, Michele Jakubowski has the teachers in her life to thank for her love of reading and writing. While writing has always been a passion for Michele, she believes it is the books she has read throughout the years, and the teachers who assigned them, that have made her the storyteller she is today. Michele lives in Powell, Ohio, with her husband, John, and their children, Jack and Mia.

About the Illustrator

Erica-Jane Waters grew up in the beautiful Northern Irish countryside, where her imagination was ignited by the local folklore and fairy tales. She now lives in Oxfordshire, England, with her young family. Erica writes and illustrates children's books and creates art for magazines, greeting cards, and various other projects.